To I. B.

—J. T.-B.

To Bunny

—E. G.

SALAAM
READS

An imprint of Simon & Schuster Children's Publishing Division
1230 Avenue of the Americas, New York, New York 10020
Text copyright © 2018 by Jamilah Thompkins-Bigelow
Illustrations copyright © 2018 by Ebony Glenn
SALAAM READS is a trademark of Simon & Schuster, Inc.
For information about special discounts for bulk purchases, please contact Simon & Schuster Special Sales at 1-866-506-1949 or
business@simonandschuster.com.
The Simon & Schuster Speakers Bureau can bring authors to your live event. For more information or to book an event, contact the
Simon & Schuster Speakers Bureau at 1-866-248-3049 or visit our website at www.simonspeakers.com.
Book design by Krista Vossen
The text for this book was set in Cabrito.
The illustrations for this book were rendered digitally.
Manufactured in China
0118 SCP
First Edition
2 4 6 8 10 9 7 5 3 1
Library of Congress Cataloging-in-Publication Data
Names: Thompkins-Bigelow, Jamilah, author.
Title: Mommy's khimar / Jamilah Thompkins-Bigelow; illustrated by Ebony Glenn.
Description: First edition. | New York : Salaam Reads, [2018] | Summary: A young Muslim girl puts on a head scarf and not only feels closer to her mother,
she also imagines herself as a queen, the sun, a superhero, and more.
Identifiers: LCCN 2016036705 (print) | LCCN 2017016421 (eBook) |
ISBN 9781534400597 (hardcover : alk. paper) | ISBN 9781534400603 (eBook)
Subjects: | CYAC: Scarves—Fiction. | Mothers and daughters—Fiction. | Imagination—Fiction. | Muslims—Fiction.
Classification: LCC PZ7.1.T4676 (eBook) | LCC PZ7.1.T4676 Mom 2018 (print) |
DDC [E]—dc23
LC record available at https://lccn.loc.gov/2016036705

Jamilah Thompkins-Bigelow   Illustrations by Ebony Glenn

Mommy's Khimar

New York London Toronto Sydney New Delhi

A khimar is a flowing scarf
that my mommy wears.

Before she walks out the door each day, she wraps one around her head.

In Mommy's closet, there are so many khimars—so many that I can't count them: black ones, white ones . . . purple, blue, and red . . . stripes, patterns, and polka dots too.

Some have tassels.

Some have beads.

Some have sparkly
things all over.

And she has my favorite color . . . yellow!

When I put on Mommy's khimar, I become a queen with a golden train.

Under the khimar, my braids and twists form a bumpy crown. It's not easy to cover the many plaits Mommy puts in my hair.

When I wear Mommy's khimar,
I shine like the sun. I dive and become
a shooting star into a pile of clouds.

Of course, I make sure that Mommy doesn't see me.

When I wear Mommy's khimar, I am a mama bird. I spread my golden wings and shield my baby brother as he sleeps in his nest.

Mommy shakes her head,
but her eyes are smiling.

When I wear Mommy's khimar, I am a superhero in a cape, dashing from room to room at the speed of light.

Daddy snatches me up and I fly.
Mommy can't stop laughing when
his bristly beard tickles my cheek
with a kiss.

When I wear Mommy's khimar, Mommy is with me even when she's away. I close my eyes and if I breathe in deeply—really deeply—I smell the coconut oil in Mommy's hair and the cocoa butter on her skin.

And if I breathe in even more deeply than that, I smell the cinnamon in her favorite dessert. She always shares a piece.

When I wear Mommy's khimar and Mom-Mom visits after Sunday service, she sings out, "Sweet Jesus!" and calls me Sunshine.

Mom-Mom doesn't wear a khimar. She doesn't go to the mosque like Mommy and Daddy do. We are a family and we love each other just the same.

When I go to the mosque wearing
Mommy's khimar, the older women coo,
"Assalamu alaikum, Little Sis!"

Mommy smiles so proud.

My Arabic teacher exclaims,
"Beau-ti-ful! Beautiful hijab!"

"Hijab" is the word she uses for "khimar." Sometimes I say "hijab" too.

When I wear Mommy's khimar and we go home and it starts to get dark outside, Mommy tells me gently, "Take it off. It's time for sleep."

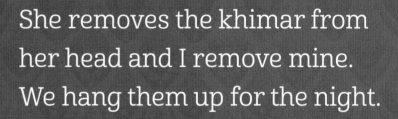

She removes the khimar from her head and I remove mine. We hang them up for the night.

I look around at all the khimars—
too many to count.

I stroke the yellow scarf one last time.

I close my eyes and breathe in deeply—really deeply. And if I breathe in deeply enough, I can take Mommy's khimar with me.

I place it inside my head. I take other things
and place them there too:

A crown with a train, the sun and
a shooting star, a baby dozing on a
golden wing.

I take a ticklish kiss in the sky, coconut and cocoa with a cinnamon sweet, and the prayers of gray-haired women.

I take all these things with me and
go to sleep. Though Mommy is away,
it feels like she comes too.